Images of New Brunswick

John Sylvester

RAGWEED
THE ISLAND PUBLISHER

For Dianne

Copyright © *John Sylvester, 1997*

All rights reserved. No part of this book may be reproduced or transmitted in any form or by any means whatsoever without permission of the publisher, except by a reviewer, who may quote brief passages in a review.

John Sylvester thanks the New Brunswick Department of Economic Development and Tourism, the management and staff of the Acadian Historical Village and Kings Landing Historical Settlement, Norma and Noël Côté of Côté's Bed and Breakfast in Grand Falls, Linda Pond of Pond's Resort in Ludlow, the staff of the Capital Theatre, Peter Clair (Biel), Bill Miller, Peter Wilcox and also his good friend Blaine Hrabi, who accompanied him on two memorable trips to Mount Carleton Provincial Park.

Front cover photograph:
The Bay of Fundy coast at Alma

Back cover photograph:
New Denmark, with the Saint John River in the background

Design by:
Janet Riopelle and Sibyl Frei

Printed and bound in Canada by:
Friesen Printers

Published by:
Ragweed Press
P.O. Box 2023
Charlottetown, PEI
Canada C1A 7N7

The French language edition of this book, *Splendeurs du Nouveau-Brunswick* (ISBN 2-7600-0332-9), is published by Les Éditions d'Acadie of Moncton, New Brunswick.

Canadian Cataloguing in Publication Data
Sylvester, John, 1955-
    Images of New Brunswick.
    ISBN 0-921556-69-1
1. 1. New Brunswick — Pictorial works. I. Title.
FC2462.S94 1997   971.5′104′0222   C97-950016-8
F1042.8.S94 1997

Preface

For a Maritimer, I've come to know New Brunswick rather late in life. It wasn't until 1988 that I first visited the province with my camera. Born in Nova Scotia, and now a resident of Prince Edward Island, I had until then only driven through New Brunswick on my way to somewhere else.

That changed with my first visit to Grand Manan Island. I was quickly seduced by its charms: fog-draped cliffs, picturesque fishing villages and friendly people. Since then I've had the good fortune to travel throughout the province. Some of the images in this book were taken while on assignment, others during solo photographic journeys or camping trips with friends and family. They represent my efforts at capturing the beauty of this remarkable place, and they hold many fond memories.

For instance, there was the June afternoon I spent on Peter Wilcox's boat, en route to the seabird colony at Machias Seal Island. Peter's father, Preston Wilcox, was on board that day. A veteran fisher and tour boat operator, he compared the experience of being on the water surrounded by thousands of calling seabirds to a great natural symphony. On that perfect afternoon, it was easy to understand what he meant.

Many months later I found myself in the cluttered shop of master canoe builder, Bill Miller. After I had spent an enjoyable afternoon photographing Bill at work, a friend and I — who were on our way to Mount Carleton Provincial Park for a few days of hiking — were invited to stay for supper. We were treated to a hearty meal of moose-meat chili and a memorable evening of music, stories and Bill's spontaneous poetry recitations.

Most recently, on a winter trip to Madawaska County, I stopped in Saint Jacques to ask for directions. The man I asked stopped shovelling snow and said, "Here, I'll show you." He got into the car with me and off we went. He told me that he had grown up in the area but moved away as a young man. Memories are strong, however, and after thirty years of living and working elsewhere he had finally come home to New Brunswick. It's the kind of place that gets in your blood, he explained, and once there it's hard to get out.

I couldn't agree more.

John Sylvester
Spring 1997

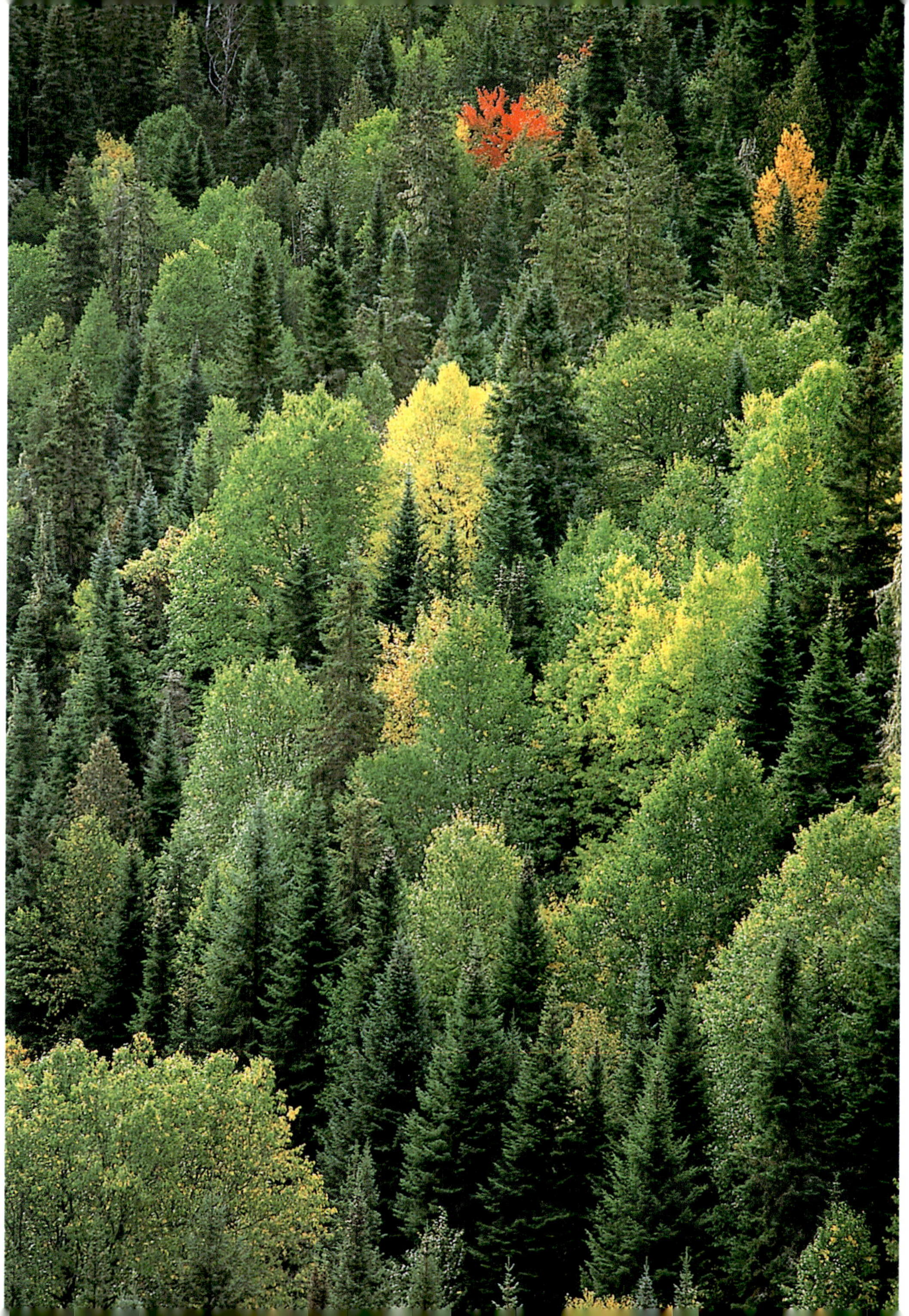

Introduction

To produce this stirring tribute to New Brunswick, John Sylvester travelled the length and breadth of the province, capturing its many landscapes and seasons. Curious, patient and blessed with a remarkable talent for observation, he has amassed an impressive collection of photographs that evoke the most meaningful aspects of a corner of the country he holds dear — an area he invites us to explore with him.

In New Brunswick, nature reigns supreme. More than 80 percent of its territory is still covered with forest, a fact that travellers discover quickly. Not only is the forest one of the mainstays of the provincial economy, it is also every nature lover's dream come true. With its countless lakes and rivers, the province is truly a paradise on earth for hikers, fishers and hunters. New Brunswick is also known for its graceful, fertile valleys, including the Saint John River basin. To view this great river is to understand why it is sometimes referred to as the "Rhine of North America." In addition, New Brunswick's 2,240 kilometres (1,390 miles) of shoreline offer majestic and beautifully diverse landscapes. In a province where no one is ever more than 180 kilometres (110 miles) from the ocean, the lobster is a "trademark" image. The spectacular tides of the Bay of Fundy to the south are an unforgettable sight, rivalled only by the sunsets on Miscou Island at the northeast.

This precious natural heritage is by no means the only source of pride for New Brunswickers. They also feel a strong attachment to their architectural heritage, to the monuments that tell their

"More than 80 percent is still covered with forest ... every nature lover's dream come true."

history. Depending on the region, New Brunswick's public buildings, humble country churches and houses bear the mark of varied influences — several periods of British architecture, including that of the Loyalists, who brought with them the American colonial style. For their part, the Acadians created an architectural style all their own, one that is found most notably in the Acadian peninsula, where brightly painted wooden houses make a striking impression on all visitors.

Forest for as far as the eye can see, beckoning valleys, the sea never more than a stone's throw away, architecture that stands as an eloquent reminder of our builders' know-how — these are but a few of the things that contribute to the charm and beauty of New Brunswick. John Sylvester has captured them all with consummate artistry and marvellous imagery. Only the proverbial hospitality with which New Brunswickers greet their visitors is missing from these pages. But that cannot be conveyed on paper. To experience it, you must set out on your own journey to discover, or rediscover, the beauty of New Brunswick, my native province.

Roméo LeBlanc
Governor General of Canada

"You must set out on your own journey to discover, or rediscover, the beauty of New Brunswick."

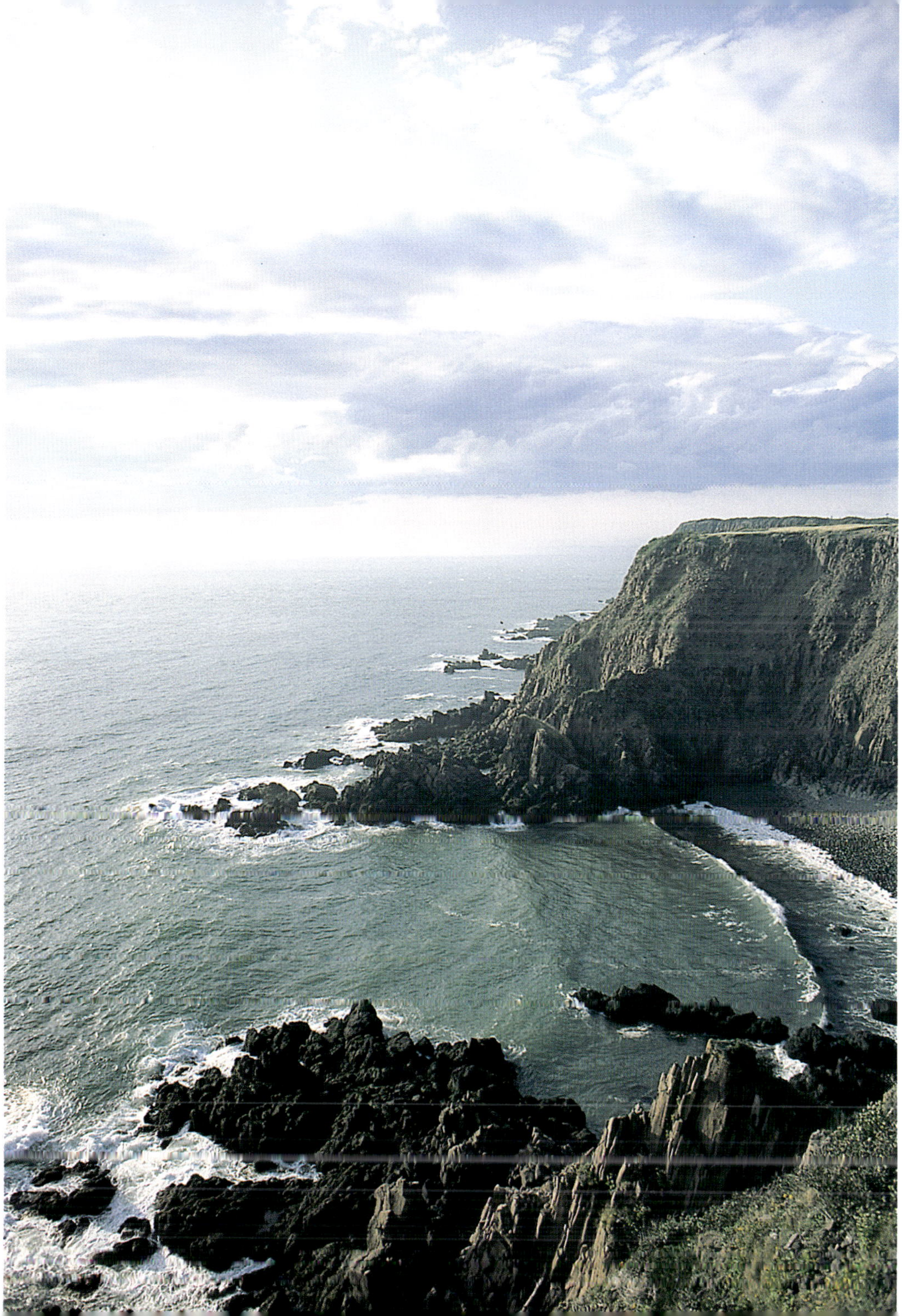

Images of New Brunswick

Opposite: Freshly painted dories capture the reflection of the setting sun.

By the Sea

Young sailors adventure in Seal Cove, blanketed by the infamous fog of Grand Manan Island, the largest of the Fundy isles.

A pair of gulls survey their surroundings from atop weathered fish sheds on Grand Manan Island.

Racks of herring dry in a smokehouse on Grand Manan Island.

East Quoddy Lighthouse, on Campobello Island, is one of Atlantic Canada's most photographed lighthouses.

Atlantic puffin, beak stuffed with brit (young herring). Several thousand seabirds nest on Machias Seal Island, a migratory bird sanctuary in the Bay of Fundy.

Sunrise highlights a herring fish weir in Passamaquoddy Bay at St. Andrews.

ocated where the Saint John River empties into the Bay of Fundy, Saint John is a port
ity first and foremost.

Saint John's Old City market offers fine food and a chance to catch up with friends old and new.

Powerful Fundy tides sculpt the mud banks of the Tantramar Marsh near Sackville.

The interior of Fundy National Park offers breathtaking natural beauty, including Third Vault Falls, the highest falls in the park.

A lone spruce stands sentinel over Chignecto Bay.

Like pebbles on the beach, semipalmated sandpipers roost on the shore at Hopewell Cape. Hundreds of thousands of these diminutive shorebirds feed on the mudflats of the upper Bay of Fundy in late July and August en route from the Arctic to South America.

Erosion caused by the incredible force of Fundy's tides has carved these cliffs at Hopewell Cape into unusual flowerpot shapes.

The Peticodiac River and its tidal flats provide the setting for the bustling city of Moncton.

Moncton's Capital Theatre first opened its doors in 1922. Lovingly restored and reopened in 1993, the new Capital recaptures the glorious atmosphere of an earlier era.

Rhodora blossoms are a sign of spring's arrival in the wetlands of eastern New Brunswick.

...adian pride is displayed on this house in Cap Pelé.

A boardwalk in Kouchibouguac National Park leads the visitor over salt marshes and lagoons to a spectacular beach.

Wintergreen leaves and lichens decorate the forest floor of Kouchibouguac National Park, which is home to more than 600 species of plants.

In 1968, Father Gerard D'Astous took his imaginative brush to the entire interior of Sainte-Cécile Roman Catholic Church in Petite-Rivière-de-l'île on Lamèque Island. Every July the church is home to the International Baroque Music Festival.

A windswept beach on Miscou Island in the far northeast of the province. One of New Brunswick's oldest lighthouses (1858) casts its warning beam to mariners on the Bay of Chaleur.

Ceasarie Ward of Miscou Island displays one of his handcrafted model ships, a two-masted fishing schooner.

New Brunswick's largest fishing fleet ties up at the wharf in Caraquet.

Young interpreters in period costume take a break at the Acadian Historical Village in Bertrand, near Caraquet. The village portrays Acadian life in the 1800s.

Stories and laughter are shared by visitors to Godin's General Store in the Acadian Village.

The old craft of hand-tying brooms continues at the Acadian Village.

A lobster boat approaches the harbour at Anse-Bleue after a morning of hauling traps in the Bay of Chaleur.

Sunset's last glow silhouettes a cormorant colony at Pokeshaw.

...storal view of the Bay of Chaleur near Stonehaven.

Opposite: Autumn transforms the province's mixed Acadian forest into a rich tapestry of colour.

On the Land

Formed of ancient granite, Mount Carleton is the highest peak in the Maritimes at 820 metres (2,690 feet). This northern provincial park features mountains, valleys, rivers and lakes in a wilderness setting.

Nictau Lake offers remarkable solitude.

From the ramparts of Mount Sagamook, a hiker surveys the spectacular view.

In the tiny community of Nictau, along the banks of the Tobique River, Bill Miller practices the canoe-building tradition for which his family is famous. Bill's grandfather turned out the first Miller canoe in 1925.

ogs piled high are a familiar sight in the province's northwest.

Casting for Atlantic salmon on the Miramichi River in the interior of New Brunswick.

A lone canoeist glides through a sunlit veil of morning mist.

A white-tailed deer raises its tail in warning; a moment later it is gone.

ray of sunlight catches the Hôtel-Dieu de Saint-Joseph spire at Saint-Basile.

Ice-fishing shacks shelter anglers during winter, even in front of the Saint Thomas D'Aquin Church on Baker Lake.

Hockey is the winter pastime of choice for youngsters in the tiny village of Moulin-Morneault.

Forestry is a central activity in Edmundston and the Madawaska region. The Cathedral of the Immaculate Conception dominates Edmundston's skyline.

Wilderness is never far in much of New Brunswick. The land reclaims its own at this abandoned farmhouse on Lake Edward.

Potatoes are the principal crop grown on these neatly tended farms in New Denmark. The first Danish settlers arrived here in 1872.

A barn mural proclaims the Danish heritage of its owners.

The coldest days of winter transform the Grand Falls gorge into a sculpture of ice and snow.

Wood weaver, Biel, practices the traditional craft of basket-making at his studio in Tobique Narrows.

A tranquil autumn evening along the Saint John River near Woodstock.

Woodstock is situated almost exactly at the half way point along the Saint John River.

Kings Landing Historical Settlement accurately portrays life in rural Loyalist New Brunswick a century ago. Here, a horsepowered treadmill is used to cut firewood.

The pace and grace of an earlier time are reflected in this woman's work at Kings Landing.

The spire of Christ Church Cathedral and the dome of the legislature building rise above the tree-lined streets of Fredericton.

Fredericton is home to the New Brunswick Legislature. Built in 1882, the sandstone structure is a fine example of Second Empire Revival style.

Rowers at sunset on the Saint John River at Fredericton.

New Brunswick tartan awaits completion at Loomcrofters Weaving Studio in Gagetown.

Charming farmsteads dot the landscape, like this one nestled in the rolling hills of Albert County.

The Smithtown Bridge, built in 1914, is one of sixteen covered bridges in Kings County, earning this county the title of "Covered Bridge Capital of Canada."

John Sylvester is a freelance photographer based in Greenvale, Prince Edward Island. His photographs have appeared internationally in numerous books, calendars and publications, including *Geo*, *Equinox*, *Canadian Geographic*, *Reader's Digest*, *Harrowsmith* and *The Globe and Mail*. His previous books include the award-winning *From Red Clay & Salt Water: Prince Edward Island & Its People* (Ragweed Press) and the children's geography book, *Canada* (MacDonald-Young).